# LUCY
## The Curiously Comical Cow

This Book Belongs To:

**Pacific Press® Publishing Association**
Nampa, Idaho
Oshawa, Ontario, Canada

Edited by Jerry D. Thomas
Designed by Robert Mason
Cover art by Mary Rumford
Inside art by Mark Ford

Copyright © 1998 by
Pacific Press® Publishing Association
Printed in the United States of America
All Rights Reserved

Vanderwerff, Corrine.
    Lucy, the curiously comical cow / Corrine
Vanderwerff.
        p.   cm. — (Julius and friends ; bk. 5)
    Summary:  A lonely girl develops an
unusual friendship with a calf that later
becomes a prize-winning milk cow.
    ISBN 0-8163-1582-5 (alk. paper)
    [1. Cows.  2. Farm life.]  I. Title.  II. Series.
PZ7.V285115Lu    1998
[Fic]—dc21                              97-32651
                                           CIP
                                            AC

98 99 00 01 02 • 5 4 3 2 1

# Contents

# Other Books in the Julius and Friends Series

Julius
Julius Again
Tina
Skeeter

# Dedication

With love to
two very special girls—
Jen and Lucy.

And with special thanks to
Heather and Greg and Kari
of Kan-Do Holsteins;
Marja and Tom and Tommy and Karen;
Dad and Bernice and Aunt Mary;
Toini;
and Date.

# About Lucy and Jen

Lucy is a special calf. Jen is a special girl. Like them, each of us is special in our own way.

God wants us to know that. He also wants us to know about the special friendship we can have with Him. In many ways, the story of Lucy and Jen is a *parable* about that kind of friendship. It makes me think of the parables Jesus told about the Shepherd and His sheep. This is part of what He said.

He calls his own sheep by name and leads them out. When he has brought out all his own, he goes on ahead of them, and his sheep follow him because they know his voice. I am the good shepherd; I know my sheep and my sheep know me—My sheep listen to my voice; I know them, and they follow me.*

As you read about Lucy and Jen, find the parts which show that kind of friendship. Would you like to have that kind of friendship with God? Talk to Him about that. Tell Him you want to be His friend. And let Him be your friend too.

Corrine Vanderwerff

*John 10:3, 4, 14, 27, New International Version

# CHAPTER
# *1*

# The Too-White Calf

The calf in the first stall stood with its legs wide apart and its head up. It lifted its freckled nose. It looked at Jen. Jen walked right by. She had come to buy a calf, and she knew exactly what she wanted. That calf would not do.

Alex tugged on her arm. "Look at that one!" she said. Jen's cousin's name was really Alexandria, but for some reason everyone called her Alex. She was pointing back at the calf in the first stall.

Jen shook her head. "It's a nice calf," she said. "But it's too white."

Uncle Lynn raised prize Holsteins and

had a first-class milking herd. Jen knew which of his cows she liked best, and she wanted a calf like them. Her calf would be black with just enough white to make it look good.

When she had first gone to live with Auntie Dawn and Uncle Lynn on the Dawn-Lynn Dairy, Jen had been afraid of cows. As far as she could tell then, all one hundred twenty-four of their Holsteins looked exactly alike. They were black and white. They were very big. They had long faces, wide ears, big eyes, funny noses, and hard, mean-looking hooves. "I'm too afraid!" she said the first time Alex had tried to get her to pet one. But all that had changed.

And now Jen went from stall to stall in the sales barn with Uncle Lynn and Alex.

Since before Christmas, she had been working hard. When news got around that she wanted to buy a calf, things began to happen. Uncle Lynn gave her chores she could do for cash. The neighbors paid her for helping at their dog kennels after school. She was even chosen to receive a gift of money from the farm group that helps kids buy their own calves. And this was the day of the special dairy calf sale for kids.

Uncle Lynn pointed out the best things about each of the calves. Some were good in one way. Some were good in another. And some were sort of just in between.

*Kind of like our family*, Jen thought. Her big brother Kenny was smart. Her little sister Rosie was cute. *But me . . . I'm just plain Jen in the middle.*

When things had gone bad at home, she had thought no one really cared about her. Her dad left and took Kenny. Mom kept Rosie with her. No one seemed sure what would happen to Jen. Then Auntie Dawn and Uncle Lynn invited her to live with them. Jen was sure they were just being nice. She thought they kept her only because they felt sorry for her.

"You want a calf that will grow up to be a good cow," Uncle Lynn said.

Jen nodded. She did want a good calf. "I think I like Blackie over there." She pointed toward a mostly black calf in the middle stall. "She's pretty."

The calf's short black hair was soft and

shiny. Its white spots were just right.

"*Mmmmmm*," said Uncle Lynn. "She's nice. But . . ." He turned. He pointed back toward the very first stall. "If I were buying a calf today, I think I would choose that one."

Jen looked. The calf in the first stall still stood with its feet wide apart and its head up. It seemed to be looking straight at her. "But it's too white," she said again. "Blackie here is prettier." She went closer to the middle stall. "It would be easier to take care of her."

By living on the Dawn-Lynn Dairy, Jen had learned many things about cows. She learned that it takes less work to keep black cows looking nice. A cow's black hair is shorter. It is easier to clean. White hair is longer. It has to be scrubbed more, and clipped. A white cow out in a field looks dirty very quickly.

Blackie stood quietly in her stall. She did not pay any attention to the people who were looking at her. She did not even seem to see Jen.

"If I were buying a calf," said Alex, "I

would choose the first one there." She pointed toward the calf her dad had picked.

Jen walked toward the first stall. "This one is nice," she said. "But she's just too white."

The calf flicked her ears.

"I think she'd make a good pet," Alex answered. "She's . . ."

But Jen was not listening. She walked back to look at Blackie.

The black calf had not moved. She still had her head down. She did not even seem to notice that Jen was there. "I don't know." Jen sounded very thoughtful. She turned and went back to the first stall.

Just then the little too-white calf pushed against the rail. She tilted her head.

"Oh, look!" Jen exclaimed. "Aren't those the cutest spots on her nose?"

"I was looking in my stockman's book," Uncle Lynn was saying. "This calf has good parents. She should make a very fine milk cow when she grows up."

Jen, though, was still not listening. She was staring at the calf's name. "Carnation Luke Clover!" She wrinkled her nose.

"That's no name. Can't you just hear me going outside and calling, 'here Carnation-Carnation-Carnation?' "

Alex giggled. "That's not her name, silly. That's the name of her farm."

The calf tossed her head. Then she tipped it and looked up at the girls with one eye. "Carnation Luke Clover is her registered name," Alex went on. "It tells where she comes from. Carnation is the name of her farm. Luke is the name of her father. And Clover is the name of her mother. You could call her Clover, after her mother."

"I'm so sure." Jen made a face. "Every farm in the country has a cow named Clover. I want . . ."

But no one heard what Jen wanted because at that very moment the calf stretched out her neck and let out a very loud and very long *maa-aaa-aaa-aaa*.

Jen smiled and reached out to pat the calf. "But I still say you're too white," she said to the little calf. "Your white spots are too big. Your black spots are too small and too crooked. You aren't like Blackie over there."

Just then the little too-white calf butted against the rail.

"Oh, you little scamp!" Jen exclaimed.

The calf pushed closer against the rail where Jen stood.

Jen reached down to pet her.

The calf looked up. She stuck out her tongue.

"Oh!" But Jen didn't say anything more. She couldn't! The little calf had her laughing too hard to talk. Alex and Uncle Lynn laughed too. "It's like she knows what I'm saying," Jen finally said when she could stop laughing. "It's like she likes me already."

"Well," asked Uncle Lynn, "now do you know which calf you want?"

"I think Blackie over there is prettier," Jen said, "But this calf is . . ." She looked down and saw the little heifer looking up at her with its big brown eyes. "This calf is special."

By the time the sale was over, the little too-white calf belonged to Jen.

Jen knelt down and stroked its soft, fluffy hair. She leaned her cheek against the calf's neck. "Carnation Luke Clover," she whispered. "Do you know what I think? I think you need a new name. And since your daddy's name is Luke, I think your name should be Lucy. Would you like to be called Lucy?"

The calf twitched her ears. She bobbed her head.

"Then from now on your name is Lucy." Jen slipped her arm over the calf's shoulder.

The calf pushed close against her.

"Oh, Lucy," Jen whispered. "I hope you like being my calf."

# CHAPTER

# 2

## Lucy Jumps
## the Gate

The rain drummed a happy *ta-ta-ti-tat ta-ta-ti-tat* on the big round roof. The milking machine sang a contented *tschoo-pumf, tschoo-pumf, tschoo-pumf*. The cows munched their grain with sniffs and soft snuffles. The barn was full of comfortable farm sounds, but Jen did not notice any of them. She did not even stop to talk with Uncle Lynn as he cleaned the next cow for the milkers. She was in a hurry to see her Lucy.

"Oh, the poor baby," she was saying to herself. "She's so alone out there."

Lucy was alone. All new calves at the

Dawn-Lynn Dairy had to stay by themselves for at least one week. That way none of the bigger animals could pick on them. That way they would not catch anything if one of the other animals was sick. And that way it would give Uncle Lynn time to see if they were sick with something that the others might catch.

"A week is too long," Jen was thinking. "I don't want her to be so alone. I don't . . ."

Jen knew all about being lonesome. She knew how it felt when she first came to stay at the farm. Everyone had been nice, but she still felt sad. And now she did not want her little calf to feel lonely. She hurried to the door that led into Lucy's part of the barn.

"Luuu-cee!" she called from the doorway. "Lucy-Lucy-Lucy!"

When she heard the shuffling of hard hooves on straw, Jen felt a quick happy feeling. She smiled. *She knows my voice already!* she thought. "Luuu-cee!" she called again. "Lucy-Lucy-Lucy!"

She heard the *scrappity-scrappity-scrape* of hard hooves against the gate.

*Oh, good, she wants to see me!* Jen thought, and she felt all tickly happy inside. She started to call again. But the scraping sound got louder. The gate began to wobble. *No, Lucy!* Jen thought. *Please don't do that!* But before she had a chance to say anything out loud, a big pink nose with black freckles pushed over the top of the gate.

"Lucy!" Jen's voice was loud.

Lucy's nose pushed further over the gate. The gate began to tip.

"Lucy! No!" Jen ran toward the gate.

The gate tipped even further.

Jen shoved her body against the gate. It felt very heavy. She pushed hard. Slowly, slowly, the gate began to move back into place. Lucy's head slid out of sight. Her hooves made a *scrape-scrape-scraping* sound along the boards. And then with a soft *ker-ploph* they dropped back onto the straw of the pen floor. Jen heard more scuffling sounds. She peeked over the gate.

Lucy stood in the center of her pen. She seemed to be waiting for Jen.

So Jen went in. "Lucy!" She tried to

sound stern. "You shouldn't do that!"

Lucy looked up with her soft, brown eyes.

Jen raised her shoulders and took a deep breath. "You look so sweet," was all she could say. "You look like you would never do anything bad. And you look like you understand everything I say. But you don't." Jen scratched her fingers along Lucy's neck. "You don't understand, Lucy. You don't know that it's too dangerous for a little calf to be out there."

Lucy pushed her neck against Jen.

"I know you like to be with me." Jen patted the calf's side. "But, Lucy, you mustn't jump over that gate. It's just too dangerous."

Jen had not told anyone yet, but on the day before, Lucy had jumped over the gate. "If you jump out of your pen again, I'll have to tell Uncle Lynn." Jen reached for Lucy's brush and began brushing her black and white coat. "And when he hears that, he won't be happy."

Jen continued to talk to Lucy. "You only have to stay in here a few more days," she said. "Then you can go to the orchard. You'll like the orchard. You'll be just outside my bedroom window."

Lucy stiffened.

Jen quickly pulled the brush back. "What is it?" she asked.

Lucy put her head down. She pointed her ears forward.

Jen watched.

Lucy took one step forward, her legs stiff.

A small furry animal hopped up on the top of the gate. Jen laughed. "Lucy," she said. "You are too curious. That's just one of the cats. You'll get used to them. They're everywhere."

That was true. A farm as big as the Dawn-Lynn Dairy needed lots of cats. And if you could get them all to stay in one place long enough, you could count at least seventeen.

Lucy kept her eyes on the cat. Suddenly she shook her head. She bounced forward on stiff legs.

The cat watched.

Lucy stretched out her neck. She reached

toward the cat with her nose.

"She's your friend," Jen was saying. But just then Lucy snorted. The cat jumped off the gate and disappeared into the barn.

Lucy stared at the spot where the cat had been. She shook her head.

"You'll get used to them," Jen said again. She'd finished brushing Lucy and went to get her lead rope. She snapped the rope onto her halter. "Come!" she said, and she began to lead Lucy around and around. "We'll do this every day." Jen talked about all the things Lucy needed to learn. "And when you're bigger, you'll be ready to go to the fair."

Before she left, Jen fed Lucy some grain. She filled her water pan. She cleaned up the dirty spots in the pen and straightened the straw. "I have to go now," she said.

Lucy followed her to the gate.

"Please, Lucy. Stay in your pen!" Jen said. She shut the gate.

There was a clattering of hooves against wood. The gate began to wobble.

"Stay down, Lucy!" Jen said sternly.

Lucy's nose pushed over the gate. And

then, before Jen could say another word, Lucy's body bumped into sight. For a moment she hung over the top like a big, lumpy, black and white sack of potatoes. Suddenly, all four hooves hit the floor. The gate snapped back into place.

For a moment, Jen didn't say anything.

Lucy pranced over to Jen. She pushed her head against Jen's side.

"This isn't good," Jen said at last. "You don't belong out here." She turned Lucy around and led her back into her pen. "Now stay there!" she said. And she ran to find Uncle Lynn.

Uncle Lynn came. He looked at the gate. He looked at Lucy. And he shook his head. "She's the first calf of her size ever to do that," he said. "We'll have to tie her up."

"No!" Jen said. "I want her to be free."

Uncle Lynn shook his head again. "She's just too smart for her own good," he said. "To keep her safe, we'll have to tie her up." And he told Jen to bring a rope.

When Jen left a few minutes later, Lucy ran after her. Before she had taken two steps, something stopped her. She looked surprised. She dug her feet into the straw. She pulled. But the rope was too strong. She could not get one step closer to the gate. She could not follow Jen.

Jen stood against the other side of the gate, watching. "The rope has to be very short, Lucy," she said. "Otherwise you could get all tangled up and get hurt very badly."

Lucy looked at Jen, and her eyes seemed to be very sad.

"I'm sorry." Jen spoke very softly. "I had to tie you up because I don't want you to hurt yourself."

As she turned and walked away, she could hear Lucy tugging at the rope. "I'll be back soon," she called.

*"Maa-aaa-aaa!"* Lucy cried. *"Maa-aaa-aaa-aaa."*

# CHAPTER

# 3

# Lucy in
# the Orchard

On the day Jen moved Lucy to the orchard, the sun was shining, the sky was blue, and the trees were pretty in their new spring-green coats. Lucy's hooves scrunched on the gravel as Jen led her along the curving farm drive. Two cats lay on the steps to the house. Lucy paid no attention to them. She walked along smartly, just as Jen had been teaching her to do.

A wire fence ran all around the orchard. Jen had already opened the gate. As she led Lucy into the orchard, she was talking. "You'll like it out here," she was saying.

"You won't have to feel so alone out here. See." She pointed toward the big yellow farmhouse. "That's my bedroom. I'll be able to watch you and talk to you right from my window."

Jen led Lucy into the shade of one of the apple trees. She was still talking when she went back to close the gate. "All of the grass here is for you," she was saying. "You can eat and eat all you want. And later there'll be apples. And pears." She kept on talking while she untied Lucy's rope. "You'll have the whole orchard just for you. And a fence that'll keep you safe."

Jen tossed the rope onto the big, flat poplar stump. She gave Lucy a playful shove. "Check it out," she said. "You're free."

Lucy seemed to understand exactly what Jen meant. She ducked her head down and kicked her back feet up. She took a few practice steps. She went farther yet. Then she saw a clump of tall grass. She stopped and looked. She began to walk stifflegged toward it. She stretched out her neck. She pushed her head into the grass. It tickled.

She snorted and backed up and shook her head. Then she stopped and stared at the grass with her ears pointed forward.

"That's just grass," Jen teased. There was a laugh in her voice. "This orchard is full of new things, Lucy. You can be as curious as you want."

Cows are curious. If they see something new in their field, they will gather around. Their eyes are not so good, but their noses are very keen. They will sniff and sniff to find out what the strange thing is. They are also curious about what is on the other side of a fence. If they can, they will push their necks through the fence to find out what's there. They will even break through the fence if they can. Loose cows can get into trouble. That is why farmers use electric fences. Uncle Lynn had put an electric fence around the orchard. He had made the gate by putting special handles on one set of wires and hooking them to the corner post by the house.

"But don't be too curious," Jen warned again. She held her hand out toward her pet and softly called, "Lucy-Lucy-Lucy."

Lucy turned. She trotted over to Jen.

"Oh, Lucy, you are so smart. You already know your name." She snapped the lead rope back onto Lucy's halter and began walking her around and around in the orchard. "If you are going to be a show calf, Lucy," Jen said, "you'll need to walk like this." She walked Lucy at just the right pace. "And you'll need to stop just right and to stand just so. You have to know how to walk backward and how to go through a narrow gate." Jen talked and talked as she walked her pet. "We'll practice every day after school," she said. "Then, when we go to the fair, you will know exactly what to do."

The afternoon slipped by and soon it was time for Jen to do her other chores. She unsnapped Lucy's rope. "I think you'll be happy out here," she said. She started walking toward the fence.

Lucy followed her.

"Stay back," Jen flapped her arms.

Lucy jumped back.

Jen turned.

Lucy skipped in a circle.

Jen ran toward the fence.

Lucy ran after her.

"No, Lucy." Jen stopped by the gate. "You have to stay in the orchard."

Lucy stopped.

Jen quickly unhooked the gate. She stepped through.

Lucy started to follow.

"No, Lucy." Jen tried to sound firm. "You have to stay in the orchard."

Lucy stopped.

Jen hooked the wires back in place.

Lucy stretched out her neck.

"NO, Lucy," Jen warned again.

Lucy stretched her neck out even farther. She took a step forward.

"I know you don't want me to go." Jen's voice was softer now. "But I have chores to do. You have to stay here by yourself for a while."

Lucy pushed her nose out further yet. The top fence wire was between her nose and Jen. Lucy seemed to be looking at the wire now. She seemed to understand that it would keep her from being with Jen. She took another step forward.

"Lucy!"Jen cried. "No! That's an electric fence. It'll . . ." But how could she make Lucy understand? Electric jolts pumped through that wire. They shocked. And electric shocks hurt sensitive little noses. She wanted Lucy to understand. But little calves aren't people. They don't learn about danger by just hearing words.

Lucy stretched out her neck even farther.

"Don't touch it, Lucy."

Lucy lifted her nose just right. She pushed it against the wire. And then she jumped. Her ears flapped up and her eyes opened wide. She stood still. She stared. And then she slowly reached her nose out again.

"Lucy!" Jen shook her head.

The tip of Lucy's nose touched the wire. She jumped. She snorted. She took several crazy steps backward. And she never touched that wire again.

# CHAPTER

# *4*

# **The Stump**

"How do you think Lucy will do at the fair?" Jen asked Alex one day.

Alex had already raised several calves. Every year she and her parents took a number of cows and calves to the fair. They always won many blue ribbons. Some of Uncle Lynn's cows had even become state champions. When other farmers saw what good cows he had, they wanted to buy his extra calves. Dairy people are always looking for good animals that will make their herds even better.

"Lucy has many good points," Alex said. "If she learns how to stand and to walk like show animals should, I'm sure the judges will like her."

"I hope so," Jen said.

Every day after school, she spent as much time as she could with Lucy. She brushed and cleaned her. She walked with her, and she fed her very well. She found that Lucy loved to eat apples. After that, she saved all the apple cores from the kitchen for her. Lucy munched them down. Sometimes Jen fed Lucy whole green apples. Lucy would take the apple with her tongue, and then crunch it with her strong back teeth.

Sometimes Jen brought Lucy a big red apple. But Lucy didn't care whether an apple was red or green because cows do not see color. They just see shapes. Sometimes Jen would show her the apple, then she would throw it far into the orchard. Lucy liked that. She would run after the apple and pick it up with her mouth. Then she would run back to Jen like a dog playing fetch. Jen tried to show Lucy how to give the apple back. But that was the part of the game Lucy did not like. She would not give up her apple. Not even for Jen. She liked apples too much. And she would stand by Jen and chomp on it with her back teeth until it cracked into little pieces and she could swallow it.

Before long, Lucy also learned to play tag. Jen would run, and Lucy would chase her. When Jen stopped and turned around, then Lucy would run and Jen would chase her.

Many times, though, Jen would just sit on the big old flat stump. Sometimes she did her schoolwork. Sometimes she wrote her thoughts in her notebook. Sometimes she just sat and petted Lucy and talked to her. One day she was studying for a test. She had a sheet of notes on her lap. Lucy ran up and pushed her head against Jen. She pushed harder and harder.

"I can't play right now," Jen said.

Lucy pushed harder yet. Jen pushed back. "I have to study," Jen said. "I have to know everything on this paper for tomorrow." She put out her foot and pushed Lucy away.

Lucy took two steps back. She tipped

her head to one side and looked at Jen. Then, before Jen could stop her, she took two quick steps forward, flicked out her long tongue, and swept Jen's study paper into her mouth.

"Oh, Lucy!" Jen yelled. "Give that back!"

But it was too late. Lucy had already eaten the paper.

One afternoon, Jen went out to the orchard and climbed onto the big stump. She kept her head down. Big tears rolled down her cheeks. She did not call Lucy. She did not say anything.

Lucy trotted over to where Jen sat. She did not jump or run like she did when she wanted to play tag. She did not butt her head against Jen's side like she did when she wanted to have an apple. She just stood very still.

"Lucy," Jen said. "Nobody understands." More tears slid down her cheeks.

Lucy stood very still and tipped her head to one side.

"Auntie Dawn and Uncle Lynn are very nice. They let me have you. And I get to see my mom and dad sometimes. But nobody really understands."

Lucy pushed her neck against Jen's side.

"Look at Alex. She knows all about taking care of calves. She knows how to feed and milk the cows. If she had to, she could run this farm all by herself."

Lucy pushed closer against Jen.

"And look at me. I can't do that. I'm not best at anything." Jen began scratching the black splotch high on Lucy's right shoulder.

Lucy began to nod her head up and down and up and down against Jen's side.

"Look at the other kids. They can all do special things." The more Jen talked, the more sorry she felt for herself. Soon she began to sob. Her tears splashed onto Lucy's shoulder.

Lucy was still rubbing her head up and down against Jen's side.

Jen gulped back a big sob. "I'm just plain Jen in the middle who isn't special about anything."

Lucy kept rubbing her head up and down and up and down. She seemed to be nodding about everything Jen said. She pushed against Jen even harder.

"Lucy, you're the only one I can talk to," Jen said between sobs.

Lucy leaned even harder against Jen. It was almost like she thought that the closer she got, the better Jen would feel.

"You're the only one who understands." She sobbed some more.

Lucy pushed harder yet.

"You're the only one who thinks I'm special."

Lucy pushed so hard that suddenly Jen felt herself sliding. She felt herself slipping over the edge of the stump. And then—*kerplomp!* Jen found herself flat on the ground. She stopped sobbing. She looked up.

Lucy's head was sticking around the side of the stump. Her eyes were big and round. Her ears stood forward.

"Oh! Lucy!" Jen cried. "You look so silly!" And then she started laughing. She laughed and laughed. "Lucy!" she said when she could talk again. "You might look silly now, but you are so smart. You know exactly what to do to make me laugh. You know exactly how to make me feel better."

Lucy tossed her head up. She whirled around.

Jen jumped up. She chased after Lucy. Lucy slid to a stop. Jen ran up to her and gave her a big hug. Lucy twisted her neck around. She looked up at Jen with one eye.

"Lucy," Jen said. "When I got you, I really wanted a black calf. I thought a black calf would be prettier. I thought a black calf would be easier to take care of. But do you know what? I like you just the way you are. You are so sweet and you are so special. I think you are the most beautiful calf I have ever seen."

# CHAPTER
# 5

# The Pop Can

Lucy loved to eat. She ate grass in the orchard. She ate hay. She ate apples. She stretched up as tall as she could and ate the leaves from the branches growing out of the old poplar stump. Whenever Jen picked things in the garden for Auntie Dawn, Lucy waited by the fence until Jen gave her something. She especially liked strawberries and nasturtiums (na-stur-shums).

Sometimes, when Jen took her out of the orchard, she even ate the dogs' food. But there was one thing that Lucy liked more than anything else, and that was her grain. She would eat as much as Jen would give her. And then she still wanted more.

"Lucy, you're getting too big," Jen sometimes teased. "You look like a soft, cuddly teddy bear. But you aren't very cuddly, and you certainly aren't soft. You are more like a giant black and white pillow. A pillow that's full of bones and muscle."

Calves do grow quickly. They can gain as much as two pounds a day. And Jen was taking such good care of Lucy that she was growing even more quickly than the other calves. By the time school was out, she weighed almost five hundred pounds. By fair time, she weighed about six hundred pounds. She stood almost as tall as Jen. By then, she had learned to walk just right. She knew how to take even steps. She knew how to stop with her front feet together and her back feet just so. She had even learned to walk backwards, and that is something cows do not like to do. But she seemed happy to do everything Jen taught her to do.

"She's almost more like a dog than a calf," said Auntie Dawn. "She comes when you call. She fetches apples that you throw. And ..." Her aunt drew a long, deep breath.

"I have just found out that she knows how to do something else." She pointed to the water faucet for the garden. The water was running. "She knows how to turn on that faucet. What is she going to do next?"

Five days later they all went to the fair. Uncle Lynn took three cows. Alex took a cow and two yearling calves. Jen took Lucy. And Auntie Dawn took all her dairy decorations to make the Dawn-Lynn Dairy cow display look good. She had dried flowers, milk cans, barn tools, and other things. She also had some posters.

Since they raised Holstein cattle, one poster told about Holsteins. This is what it said.

HOLSTEIN CATTLE

Holsteins are usually black and white.
No two cows have exactly the same shape of spots.
Their real name is Holstein-Friesian.
They first came to America from Holland.
They are the biggest dairy cows.

They all worked hard. Every morning and every evening, Uncle Lynn took his milk cows to the fair milking parlor. It had big glass windows so the fair visitors could watch the farmers milk. All day, every day, Jen and Alex worked hard to keep their display clean. That many animals in a small place can make a lot of messes, and it seemed like they always had to be scooping up from behind one cow or the other.

The first day of the fair was very hot. It got hotter. Alex and Jen washed their calves to cool them off, then they took them back into the barns. Alex moved their big electric fans so they would keep the animals more comfortable. But it was so hot that not even Lucy was frisky. She stood very quietly in the corner where Jen had tied her.

The day got even hotter than ever. The girls made sure the animals had plenty of water to drink. It was so hot they drank lots of water themselves. They bought cans of ice cold pop. Jen sipped her pop.

Lucy watched. She swished her tail.

Jen set the half-full can on the top of the stall wall.

Lucy watched. The can was just above her head.

Jen went to get a brush from their box. Lucy had a dirty spot on her back.

Lucy watched Jen turn her back. Then she lifted her head. She reached out her tongue. She curled it around the can of pop. She tipped the can forward. She pulled it between her lips. Then she tipped back her head.

"Jen!" Alex called.

Jen turned. Alex was pointing at Lucy.

"What?" Jen did not know what else to say. Lucy's head was tilted back. She held the pop can in her mouth. Jen could see her swallowing as the pop ran down her throat. "I told you," she said to Alex. "She thinks she's a person. She tries to do everything she sees us do."

Just then Lucy dropped her head down. She let the empty pop can fall on the straw.

"I wonder if she would do that again?" Alex asked.

The girls looked at each other. They

grinned. Jen picked up the pop can and filled it with water. "Here, Lucy-Lucy-Lucy," she called. She held the can up high.

Lucy lifted her head. She opened her mouth. Jen popped the can between her lips. Lucy tipped her head back and let the water run down her throat.

"Look at that!"

Jen heard a voice behind her.

"Does your cow always drink pop?"

Jen shook her head. "It's water," she said. "But she just drank my can of pop."

"Have you ever seen the like?" another passerby said. "Imagine. A cow drinking out of a pop can! How did you teach her to do that?"

Jen shrugged. "Lucy's special," she said. "She tries to do everything she sees us do. I left my can of pop there on the wall. She took it and drank it just like she's seen me do."

Word got around that there was a pop-drinking calf at the Dawn-Lynn Dairy display. People came to see. Lucy drank can after can full of water.

"Aren't you afraid she'll drink too much?"

someone asked.

"I doubt that we can give her too much water." Alex liked to talk to people about their cows. "Cows need lots of water. A milking cow needs to drink at least four or five gallons of water for every gallon of milk she gives. That's up to 50 gallons, or 800 glasses, of water every day. Lucy's not a cow yet—she's only eight months old. But she already weighs almost six hundred pounds. She needs lots of water."

When she finished the pop can of water that Jen had just given her, Lucy tilted her head as if she were listening to Alex too. The black freckles on her nose stood out. The black patches around her eyes made her look like she was watching everything.

"May I pet her?" a little boy asked.

"Sure," Jen said. "She likes to be petted."

"What else can she do?" someone else asked.

Jen laughed. "Well, she does some things that most cows don't do. She can turn on a water faucet. She plays tag. She bobs for apples in a pail of water. And she comes

4—LUCY

when I call her name."

"My, what a smart calf!" someone said.

Jen felt very pleased at the attention Lucy was getting. She nodded her head. "Yes," she said. "She's very smart, and she's full of surprises. We never know what she might do next."

# CHAPTER

# 6

# Lucy on the Loose

After Lucy had her bath the next morning, Jen tied her outside by the wash rack. "Be a good girl," she said. She gave her a quick hug, patted her side, then went to wash one of Uncle Lynn's cows.

As always, Jen had wrapped Lucy's rope around the rail and looped the end into a careful slip knot. She did not like to tie up her pet, but she had to. That was one of the fair rules. Besides, if Lucy were not tied, she would follow Jen everywhere. And having a calf following you through the crowds at a large fair can be very unhandy. It can be even more unhandy when that calf already weighs 600 pounds and is almost as big as a full-grown cow.

All the cows and calves at the fair were tied up the same way. That kept them where they belonged. It also kept them safe. In case of a fire or other danger, anyone could easily untie them. A quick tug on the end of the rope would slip the knot loose and the animal could be quickly led to safety.

Lucy watched Jen wash Uncle Lynn's cow. She tipped her black ears forward as though listening for Jen to say something. But Jen kept her back turned. She was too busy scrubbing the other cow to talk to Lucy. Suds foamed up around the scrub brush. Lucy watched a little longer. Jen seemed to have forgotten all about her. Lucy tossed her head to one side as if to say, "Well, OK for you too." But she did not snort through her nose. She did not stretch her neck forward and let out a loud *Maa-aaa-aaa* like she did when she wanted Jen's attention. Instead, she opened her mouth and stuck out her tongue.

Now, like all cows, Lucy has a tongue that

is long and rough and strong. A cow can do many things with her tongue. In fact, she can use it almost like we use our hands. It is just right for eating grass. It is just right for sweeping up a good mouthful of hay. It is just right for picking up many things. Lucy had already learned to do many things with her tongue, and now she did not reach for a clump of grass. She did not try to get some hay. Instead, she was looking at something else. She was looking at her rope.

With a quick flick, Lucy folded her tongue around the end of her rope.

No one saw what she was doing. No one stopped her. No one said anything at all.

Lucy tilted her head up. She pulled on the rope just like Jen always did. And just like it always did for Jen, the knot in the rope popped loose. Lucy dropped the rope. She turned. She took a few careful steps. And then she was on her way.

All the while, Jen was busily scrubbing the other cow. She did not see her pet turn. She did not see the rope dragging on the ground. She did not know that Lucy was loose.

Lucy held her head up just as Jen had taught her to do. She walked with the careful sway of a teenage heifer calf who knows where she's going. As a matter of fact, she did know. And she turned toward the lawn beside the cattle barns. It had beautiful green grass, some pretty shade trees, and was a favorite picnic spot for visitors to the fair. Many people sat on the grass. Lucy turned toward a group of teenagers who were drinking pop. She started to walk faster.

"Look!" A boy pointed toward Lucy.

A girl with long blond hair turned just as Lucy stretched her head forward. But instead of sharing her pop, the girl screamed. In the next moment, people all over the lawn were jumping to their feet. The kids with the pop started running. Lucy hurried after them.

"Loose cow!" someone yelled.

Jen looked quickly around. She saw the people running. She heard them yelling, "Go away! Go away!"

In the middle of everything, Jen saw a swaying black and white behind. She saw a white tail swish into the air. She looked back to where Lucy was supposed to be. Her mouth fell open.

"Jen! Jen!" she heard Alex calling just then. "Quick! Lucy's loose!"

"Catch that cow!" someone else yelled.

Jen saw three men chase after Lucy. From the way Lucy kicked up her back feet and spurted ahead, Jen could tell that Lucy thought they were playing. *Oh dear!* she thought. *She thinks this is a game of tag!*

Lucy kept ahead of the men. She ran faster. She had become 600 pounds of bouncing black-and-white energy running away from the men. And running toward the food stands. Straight in front of her stood the fancy table where the dairy women were selling ice cream and chocolate milk. Beside them, someone else was selling pop.

"Catch her! Catch her!" the women yelled.

A man in a gray suit and a big cowboy hat grabbed for her rope. But Lucy was too quick. She tossed her head, and the man did not get her rope. She kept running toward the dairy stand.

"Oh, dear," Jen dropped the wash bucket. "What shall I do?"

A boy in purple shorts jumped in front of Lucy.

"Stop her!" the people called. "Stop her!"

Lucy did not stop. She did not turn. She kept running as if she were going to run right through the boy. Just in time, he jumped out of her way.

Jen started to run too. What if Lucy smashed down the tables? What if she spilled all the chocolate milk? What if she tried to get the pop? But Jen did not have time to catch her. No way could she run fast enough. So she stopped. She took a big, deep breath and then called out in her very loudest voice, "Luuu-cee!"

Lucy flicked her ears.

"Luuu-cee!" Jen called again.

Lucy braked all four feet at once.

"Lu-cy-Lu-cy-Lu-cy!"

Lucy slid to a stop. She turned.

"Lu-cy-Lu-cy-Lu-cy!" Jen's voice was quieter now. She called to Lucy like she always did.

Lucy began trotting toward Jen.

All the people stopped. They watched, their eyes round, as if they could not believe what they were seeing. They did not say anything.

Lucy trotted right up to Jen and pushed her head against Jen's shoulder. Jen patted her on the side of her neck. "Good girl, good girl," she said.

"Is she yours?" someone finally asked.

Jen nodded. She slipped her arms around Lucy and gave her a quick hug.

"I've never in the world seen anything like that," someone else said. "Does she always come when you call?"

Jen nodded again.

People shook their heads. "Imagine! A runaway cow! Stopping when she hears her name!"

"How did you teach her how to do that?" someone else asked.

Jen shrugged. "I take good care of her," she finally said. "She knows my voice and she always comes when I call her name. I guess she knows that I love her."

# CHAPTER

# 7

# Biter

Lucy flicked one ear. She swished her tail. She shifted her feet.

"It's OK!" Jen was saying. She leaned against Lucy's shoulder. "You did your best. Besides, you already have some blue ribbons."

Lucy stood very still now.

"You don't always have to be in first place." Jen was looking at the basket on the wall.

It was already the third day of the fair and a rainbow of ribbons hung over the edge of the basket in Auntie Dawn's display. They were the prize ribbons the Dawn-

Lynn cattle had already won. Many of the ribbons were blue. Some were white. Some were red. A beautiful purple rosette lay on top. That was for Uncle Lynn's champion cow. And one lonely green ribbon stuck out among the others.

"Somebody had to be in sixth place," Jen was saying. But she did not add that there had been only six calves in that show. Instead, she went over and pulled the green ribbon from the basket.

"Is that the cow that ran away?"

Jen turned. A little girl was looking at Lucy. A man with a video camera stood beside her. "Is she yours?" the girl added.

Jen nodded.

"Is it all right if I pet her?"

"Sure," Jen said. "Lucy likes to be petted." She took an apple from a bucket. "Lucy likes apples too," she said. "Would you like to give her one?"

The little girl smiled. She took the apple. Some other people stopped to watch.

"Just hold it out to her," Jen was saying. "She'll be gentle."

The man with the camera took two

steps back. He started filming the little girl as she fed the apple to Lucy. "Oh!" the little girl said when Lucy took the apple. "This is fun. I like her!"

More people had gathered by then. They petted Lucy. They fed her more apples. They had their pictures taken with her too.

"See, Lucy," Jen said. "Everyone likes you. They like you just the way you are, even if you were only in sixth place in the last show." Jen held up the green ribbon.

Suddenly Lucy swiped her tongue out, and before Jen knew what she was doing, she pulled her ribbon into her mouth.

"Look at that!" More people were pointing at Lucy. "She just ate her ribbon!"

"Oh!" said the first little girl who fed her the apple. "Someday when I get a cow, I want her to be just like Lucy."

Other visitors at the fair said the same thing. They wanted to buy calves just like Lucy. They liked the things she did. They said she was very special and that even if she did not get a first place ribbon in every show, she would still be a good cow when she grew up.

Lucy was growing up, and after the fair things would be changing for her and Jen. In a few weeks she would have to go to the field with the other calves who had grown too big for their pens. Just thinking about that gave Jen a crunchy feeling inside. One part of her didn't want Lucy to grow up. Another part looked forward to the time that Lucy would be a milking cow.

Two or three months past her second birthday, Lucy would have her first baby calf. That would make her a milk cow. Then she would be part of Uncle Lynn's milking herd. Jen and Uncle Lynn would carefully choose the father for her calves so that they would also be prizewinning stock. Every year after that, she would have another calf. Jen could keep some if she wanted. She could sell the others. That way Lucy would help her to have money for going to college. "Oh, Lucy," Jen said. "You are such a special pet."

After the fair, Uncle Lynn needed to go to the farm where Lucy had been born. He invited Alex and Jen to go along. "Maybe you can see Lucy's mother there," he said.

At the farm, the girls talked to two of the farmhands. "Do you have a cow named Clover?" Jen asked.

"Clover?"

Both girls nodded, and Alex told the men Clover's full name.

"I bought her baby at the calf sale for kids," Jen said.

"*Ohhhh!*" Said one of the men. "So you have Biter's calf."

Jen looked at Alex. Alex looked at Jen. "Biter?" Both girls asked at once.

The men nodded. "Yup!" said the first man. "Biter." He looked at the other farmhand. "S'pose it wouldn't hurt to take these kids to see Biter," he said.

" S'pose it wouldn't," said the other.

"Well, then . . ." He waved for the girls to follow. "Old Biter's quite a cow," he said. "Never get more 'n one like her on a farm."

*Never get more than one like Lucy, either*, Jen was thinking.

"Sometimes you'd swear she thinks just like a person. Like that day when that man came to visit. I dunno what it was that Biter didn't like about him. But when he

5—LUCY

turned his back and started to walk away, she just kinda sneaked after him. All of a sudden, she stretched her neck out, opened her mouth up big, and bit him right on the bottom. Here," he said pointing into the loafing pen. "That's Biter over there. Wanna go in and see her closer?"

Jen looked at Alex.

Alex tipped her head like she did when she was thinking. "If she bites people, then I think I'd like to stay on this side of the fence," she said.

"Yeah," said Jen. "We'll just look at her from here."

Watching Biter, Jen felt almost as if she were looking at another Lucy. Biter held her head in that certain way and she had that certain look about her eyes. "She's Lucy's mother, all right," both of the girls said. "And Lucy looks just like her."

"Only Lucy doesn't bite," said Jen.

That week Jen's mother came to visit. She took Jen for a long drive. They talked and talked. Jen told her about Lucy and about some of the crazy things she did. "At the last fair she got an award for being All-

State Calf," she said. "But she doesn't always get first place. Once she was even last. A lot of the time she's sort of just in the middle." *Kind of like me,* Jen was thinking, but she didn't say that out loud. Instead she said, "But she's still special."

"I can tell that you take very good care of your Lucy," her mother said. "I'm sure that's why she's learned to do so many fun things. You have a talent for working. And I am proud of how well you are doing here on the farm. Even though you live here now, there is one thing I want you always to remember. No matter where you are and no matter who takes care of you, you will always be mine—all mine. You are my special Jen."

"Yeah," was all Jen said. She could not think of anything else to say. Not then.

# CHAPTER
# 8

# The Backdrop

Jen sat on her bed staring outside. She had already finished her morning chores. And now rain streamed against the window making everything outside look like uneven blobs of green and gray. She saw Lucy huddled under the biggest apple tree. She did not worry about her though. Cows were built to be in the rain. Instead she was thinking about what would happen after the next fair. Just then she heard the *tinging* sound of pans being set on the stove. She pushed herself off the bed and went to the kitchen.

"I'll set the table, if you like," she offered.

"Thanks," Auntie Dawn said. She poured pancake batter into the frying pan. Uncle Lynn liked to have a big breakfast after he came in from milking.

Jen quickly set out four plates and put the knives and forks in neat lines beside them. "Do you think it'll stop raining before the fair?" she asked.

"Probably," her aunt said absentmindedly. "Which reminds me. I've just thought of a new idea for a backdrop." Auntie Dawn was always getting ideas for making things, and now she started telling Jen what she wanted to do for the next fair. "I'll sew two black bedsheets together, stitch on some red-felt letters, and then if you and Alex will make some new white posters . . ."

While her aunt talked, Jen could almost see the long black cloth with white spots and big red letters saying DAWN-LYNN DAIRY.

"And we could use it year after year."

Just then Uncle Lynn and Alex came in. Soon they were all making plans for the next fair. They were so busy talking that Jen almost forgot about what had been bothering her.

On the morning before the fair was to begin, her aunt and uncle went to the fairgrounds to put up their new backdrop. Uncle Lynn brought a ladder so he could put it up high on the wall. "How's that?" he asked.

"Looks great!" Auntie Lynn said. "No cow will ever be able to reach that."

That afternoon they brought their animals. After spending most of the year out in their fields, some of the older fair cows had become rather jumpy. If a stranger suddenly touched them from behind, they could easily become frightened. They might even kick. Uncle Lynn and Auntie Dawn did not want anyone to be hurt, and they knew just what to do. They put Lucy at the first corner of their display. Lucy was gentle. She liked people, and she loved to be petted. And the visitors loved Lucy. They petted her. They fed her apples. They had their pictures taken with her. They also said many nice things about the new backdrop. The judges liked it, too, and they gave Auntie Dawn a big blue ribbon for it.

The posters the girls had made told many things about dairies and about cows. When people asked questions, Alex was always ready to tell them more. She knew lots of interesting facts about cows.

"There is one milk cow for every six people in the United States," she might say. "A Holstein cow gives about eight gallons of milk a day. That's enough for 128 people to each have one glass of milk."

Or she might say, "A cow spends lots of time eating—up to eight hours per day. Some people say a cow has four stomachs. Actually she has one stomach with four compartments."

Or she might say, "Cows have thirty-two teeth, but they don't have any front teeth on top. In their place, they have a tough pad of skin. They do have bottom teeth all around and big grinding teeth in back on both top and bottom."

Several times each day, the girls took away the dirty straw from behind their animals. They cleaned out the wet straw. Then they piled in fresh, clean straw, spreading it over the old straw that did not need to be taken away. Each time they added new straw, the bed on the floor got higher and higher. "You're such a good helper, Jen" Auntie Dawn said one evening. "I don't know how we would ever manage without you."

When her aunt said that, Jen felt very good. It made her want to work even harder.

Finally it was the last day of the fair. The girls cleaned away the wet and dirty bedding one more time and added another layer of fresh straw. They spread it under the animals, tucking it neatly around the edges like they always did. Then they went to visit some of the other displays.

Auntie Dawn stayed in the barn office just across from their display. She could watch the animals from there. The cows munched their hay. Lucy stood in her corner. She lazily switched her tail and seemed to be happily eating. Someone stopped to chat with Auntie Dawn. Suddenly there was a loud tearing noise. Auntie Dawn jumped. She looked across at their display. "Lucy!" she cried.

At the sound of her name, Lucy twisted

her head around. There was another loud tearing sound.

"Stop!" Auntie Dawn yelled.

Lucy shook her head. Something long and black fluttered from her mouth.

Auntie Dawn ran toward where Lucy stood.

Lucy looked at Auntie Dawn. Her eyes were soft and gentle. But her mouth was chewing up and down. She was chewing on the corner of a giant piece of black cloth with red letters.

Auntie Dawn looked at Lucy. She looked up at the wall. "My backdrop!" was all that she could say. Just then Jen and Alex came.

"Oh no!" said Alex.

Jen did not say anything. She looked at Auntie Dawn. She looked at Lucy. And she looked up at where the backdrop should be. Half of it dangled from the wall. The other half dangled from Lucy's mouth. "Oh! No!" she finally said.

Lucy flicked her ears. She chewed on the cloth.

Jen reached for Lucy's halter with one

hand. With the other she grabbed her lower jaw.

Lucy opened her mouth. The backdrop dropped to the straw. Auntie Lynn grabbed it up.

Lucy rolled her eyes upward. She tried to pull away from Jen. She stuck out her tongue.

"Oh no you don't!" Jen said. She held fast to the halter so Lucy could not reach the rest of the backdrop and pull it off the wall.

"I thought you put the backdrop up high enough so none of the cows could reach it," Alex was saying to her mother.

Auntie Dawn found her tongue at last. "We did put it high enough," she said. But there is one thing we did not think about." She pointed to the floor of the stall. "All the clean straw we've added has made the cows' bed higher. And that . . . that . . . that terrible Lucy . . ."

Lucy looked at Jen.

"And now look at my backdrop. After all my work." Auntie Dawn did not sound happy.

Lucy pushed her head against Jen's side.

"This is not good," Jen said.

Lucy began to rub her head up and down.

"What you did is very bad," Jen said. "Auntie Dawn is not happy. I am not happy."

Lucy pushed even harder against Jen.

"I know you didn't mean to make us unhappy," Jen said now. "And I know you didn't know any better. But, Lucy!" She flopped her arms around her pet's neck. "You are such a mischief. What am I ever going to do with you? When will you ever grow up?" The minute she said that, Jen suddenly got the yucky, crunchy feeling that had been bothering her lately. She knew very well what was going to have to happen. And she didn't like it at all.

# CHAPTER

# *9*

# **Lucy and Buddy**

Less than two weeks after the fair, it was time for school to start again. Lucy was too big to stay in the orchard any longer. She was too little to go to the main pasture with the milk cows. The time Jen was worrying about had come.

"She needs to go to the other farm," Uncle Lynn said one morning.

Jen suddenly felt all crunchy inside again. "I wish she didn't have to," she said.

"She needs to be with other animals," said her uncle.

The Dawn-Lynn Dairy is big, but there's only enough land at the main farm for the milking cows and the young calves. The yearlings, those almost-grown animals under two years old, stayed at *the other farm*. That's what they called their big pastures a few miles down the road from the main farm. There the yearlings got used to being outside with other animals. There they had lots of room. And there they had plenty of grass to eat.

Twice a week Uncle Lynn drove over to make sure the yearlings had enough hay in the open shed. If they wanted to, they could even go under the shed when it rained.

"Lucy'll be terribly lonely over there," Jen was saying.

"She needs to be with other animals," Uncle Lynn said.

"But she thinks she's a person," said Jen. "She'll miss me."

Uncle Lynn nodded. "Lucy is special," he said. "But it's time for her to learn that she is growing up to be a cow. It'll be easier for her if she learns that now."

"I know," Jen said. But inside she was thinking, *It won't be the same*. She didn't say anything out loud about that or about how she felt on the inside. She didn't say that she wished Lucy didn't have to grow up. And how she wished that all their good times could just go on forever.

"We all have to grow up sometime," Uncle Lynn was saying. He was always very practical.

Auntie Dawn had joined them. "Growing up can be fun," she said. "You get to do new and different things. Besides, you'll still be able to go over to spend time with her."

And so it was that Lucy moved to the other farm.

On the days that Jen visited, Lucy always hurried over to see if she had brought some grain. No matter how much grass she ate—and cows love to eat grass—she always had room for grain. And she still liked to be petted. But Jen could tell that she also liked being with the other animals.

Then one day Uncle Lynn needed to move the yearlings to another pasture with more grass. He brought along Buddy, his cow dog. Buddy was a border collie. His job was to herd the cows. Uncle Lynn had trained him well, and he knew just what to do. He got behind the yearlings and began to move them toward the gate.

Most of the other yearlings were not show animals like Lucy. They did not know about walking just so or about going through gates. But when Buddy got behind them, it was like having two people showing them what to do. And they walked along in the right direction, grabbing a bite of grass here and another there. Before long, Buddy had them moving right through the opening and into the other field. That is, he had all of them moving except for one.

Lucy kept munching grass right where she was.

She did not pay any attention to the other yearlings. She did not pay any attention to Buddy. She did not pay any attention to Uncle Lynn or even to Jen. Jen had brought her some apples, and she had already eaten them. And now she was happy just to eat more grass.

Suddenly Buddy noticed that Lucy was not with the others. He stopped. He turned. He started to go around her like a good cow dog should.

Lucy saw Buddy making a wide circle. She turned her head to see him better. But she did not move. Instead, she put her head down and swiped up another three bites of grass.

Buddy took four steps toward Lucy.

Lucy still did not move.

Buddy stopped. This cow did not seem to be very smart. She did not know what she was supposed to do. He started to circle around her again.

Lucy took one step in Buddy's direction. Then she reached down and swiped up another mouthful of grass.

Buddy did his best to turn her in the right direction.

But Lucy did not turn. Instead, she lifted her head and watched Buddy.

He took a few careful steps in her direction.

Lucy still did not move.

Buddy stopped. He seemed to be wondering what to do now.

Suddenly Lucy put her head down. She started toward Buddy.

Buddy took a quick step back.

Lucy walked faster. She headed straight for him.

Buddy watched with surprised eyes. This was not going right.

By then Lucy was running. She was big, much bigger than she had been at the fair. And she was running as if she never planned to stop.

Suddenly Buddy let out a surprised yip. He fell backward—*plop!* Right on his bottom. And then he spun around and started to run.

Lucy ran faster yet. At last, the dog was playing like he was supposed to.

Buddy galloped away full speed.

Lucy chased after him. This dog knew how to play tag after all.

Buddy ran faster yet, much faster than Lucy. He was heading straight for Uncle Lynn.

Lucy followed.

Buddy swerved. He ducked behind Uncle Lynn's legs.

Lucy was pounding straight toward them.

He peeked around Uncle Lynn's legs.

At the last moment Lucy stopped.

Buddy stood very still.

Lucy looked at the dog. She waited. But Buddy did not move.

"Lucy," Jen called. "Come, Lucy-Lucy-Lucy!"

When Lucy heard Jen's voice, she turned and went over to where Jen stood.

"Oh, Lucy," Jen said. "Dogs herd cows. They don't play tag." Then Jen spoke more softly. "That looked so funny," she said. "But never mind. You'll soon get used to doing things with the other animals." She patted Lucy's neck. "C'mon," she said. "Let's go."

Buddy watched from behind Uncle Lynn's legs. Uncle Lynn said something to him, and he wagged his tail. But Lucy paid no attention now. She was following Jen. Together they walked through the gate and into the other field. And soon Lucy was where she belonged, happily eating grass with the other yearlings.

"When it's fair time next year, do you think she'll remember how to be a show animal?" Jen asked Uncle Lynn later.

"Cows are smarter than many people think," Uncle Lynn answered. "I'm sure Lucy will remember. I think that when she hears your voice and knows that you are beside her, she will always try her best to do exactly what you want her to do."

# CHAPTER
# *10*

## Skye

Another year went by, and Lucy was back at the main farm. When Uncle Lynn came into the house one morning, he called Jen. "It's a heifer!" he said. "A little girl calf!"

Jen hurriedly pulled on her boots and ran out to the calving pen. Lucy stood by the rail. Beside her stood a little black and white calf with wobbly legs braced far apart. Lucy looked down at her baby. She made a soft *moo*ing sound.

"Oh, Lucy, she's beautiful!" Jen cried.

The calf wagged her little tail. She butted her head against her mother. Most new-born calves do that when they want milk. But there was something special about the way this little one was acting. Jen knew exactly what it was. "Lucy," she said. "She's perfect. She's just like you." She chattered on, her voice happy. "You're both perfect. And do you know what? I'm going to name your baby Skye. Don't you think that's a good name?"

Lucy bobbed her head up and down like she usually did when Jen talked to her.

Now that Lucy was a mother, she had become a milk cow. She was part of the Dawn-Lynn Dairy herd. When Lucy was ready to go out to the pasture with the other cows, Jen took Skye to the special pen for newborns.

"I'll take good care of you," she whispered to Lucy's baby. "I'll make sure you get just the right kind of milk. I'll make sure that you aren't lonely. I'll make sure that you have the best of everything." And every morning and every evening Jen brought little Skye a big, square bottle full of the best milk. And every morning and every evening Skye sucked happily on the bottle's big nipple. Soon she was eating grain too. She grew quickly. The more she grew, the more she was like her mother.

And then it was summer.

Uncle Lynn and Auntie Dawn were away for the day. By then, Alex had become an expert milker. She was in charge while her parents were gone. Jen was her helper. Cows don't like to have just anybody helping at milking time, but they liked Jen.

Uncle Lynn's milking area had room for only four cows at a time. As usual, Lucy came with the others, but she was never in a hurry. She poked here and she poked there, looking at this and looking at that. At last she took her place in the milking line. And, as usual, she was the very last one. When it was finally her turn, she went in and Jen washed her.

Jen pushed the button on the feeder. Lucy's grain dumped in. Lucy pushed her nose into the feeding pan. She hurriedly scooped up mouthful after mouthful of her grain. Then she licked her tongue around the pan to be sure to get every bit.

"Lucy!" Jen suddenly exclaimed.

"Whatever's happened?" But Jen was not paying any attention to Lucy's face or to her food. She was staring at her behind. "Where is your tail?"

Lucy did not look up. She was too interested in getting every piece of grain. But she did swish her tail. It slap-slapped from side to side. Only now it looked like a short piece of dirty white rope. The beautiful, long brush of white hair was gone.

Alex came to put the milkers on Lucy. She, too, stopped and stared. "Where's her tail?" she exclaimed.

Jen shrugged. "She's so curious. She must have wandered off somewhere and got it caught on something."

By then Alex had the milkers on Lucy.

The milking machine sang a happy *tschoo-pumf, tschoo-pumf, tschoo-pumf* as the milk swished through the long hoses and into the big milk tank.

Three cats marched back and forth on the rail above the milking place.

The barn was full of the smell of fresh milk and new hay.

Jen reached through the bars to scratch

Lucy's shoulder. "She doesn't look so good without her tail, does she?" She was asking Alex. "I wonder if it'll grow back?"

Alex, though, could not say for sure.

A few weeks later when the evening milking was finished, Jen filled some grain into a bucket. All the cows had gone out to their pasture, but she called Lucy back. By then the hair had started to grow back at the end of Lucy's tail, and it was starting to look better.

Jen set the feed bucket to the side.

"Lucy," she said, "I'm so proud of you. Not many cows are good enough to be in Uncle Lynn's herd. And your Little Skye is so much like you."

Lucy lifted her head, and Jen patted her face.

"Oh, Lucy." She slipped an arm across Lucy's shoulder. "You are so special. I'll never forget all the fun we've had. And next year I want all of us to go to the fair. You and Skye and me." She leaned against Lucy's side and felt Lucy pushing back like she always had. "You've been so good for me. You always listen when I need to talk.

You've helped me to know that I'm not just Jen in the middle."

She was whispering, and Lucy flicked her ears like she always did.

"I know now that I'm special too. Both of us are—you and me. We're both important to the Dawn-Lynn Dairy team. Even though you wrecked Auntie Dawn's backdrop, you're still their favorite fair cow. And I'm such a good helper they don't have to hire someone extra when they go away."

Jen drew a deep breath. "We're both growing up, Lucy. I've got to go back to school tomorrow. You're a working cow. And soon I'll need to start training little Skye to be a fair calf."

Jen leaned her head against the cow's warm shoulder. Suddenly she was remembering what her mother had said. And then she heard herself saying those very same words. Only now she was saying them to Lucy. "No matter what happens or who takes care of you, Lucy, I'll never forget you. You'll always be mine—all mine." Jen let her arm rest on Lucy's shoulder, and the cow turned and snuggled her head against

Jen. "You are so special. Lucy, you've been better than a best friend."

She hugged Lucy again, and then she set the bucket of grain where Lucy could reach it. After giving her pet another pat on the neck, she stepped back to let Lucy eat.

Lucy's ears twitched like they always did when she was happy. The rest of her face was pushed into the bucket right up to her eyes. Her eyes, though, were watching Jen, and Jen saw her close one in what looked exactly like a slow wink.